For beloved Ganittha. In tranquility, 1971-1990 — W.P.C.

To all the kids who call me Auntie or Grandma — M.L.

Adventures in Storytelling

Kao and the Golden Fish

A Folktale from Thailand

As Remembered by Wilai Punpattanakul-Crouch

Retold by Cheryl Hamada
Illustrated by Monica Liu

 **CHILDRENS PRESS** ®
CHICAGO

An Introduction to Storytelling

By Janice M. Del Negro

*O*nce upon a time . . . .

These are magic words. They open kingdoms and countries beyond our personal experiences and make the impossible possible and the miraculous, if not commonplace, at least not unexpected.

Before video recorders, tape recorders, television, and radio, there was storytelling. It was the vehicle through which every culture remembered its past and kept alive its heritage. It was the way people explained life, shared events, and entertained themselves around the fire on dark, lonely nights. The stories they told evoked awe and respect for tradition, ritual, wisdom, and power; transmitted cultural taboos and teachings from generation to generation; and made people laugh at the foolishness in life or cry when confronted by life's tragedies.

As every culture had its stories, so too did each have its storytellers. In Africa they were called griots; in Ireland, seanachies; in France, troubadours; and in the majority of small towns and villages around the world they were simply known as the gifted. Often their stories were hundreds of years old. Some of them were told exactly as they had been told for centuries; others were changed often to reflect people's interests and where and how they lived.

With the coming of the printing press and the availability of printed texts, the traditional storyteller began to disappear — not altogether and not everywhere, however. There were pockets in the world where stories were kept alive by those who remembered them and believed in them. Although not traditional storytellers, these people continued to pass down folktales, even though the need for formal, professional storytelling was fading.

In the nineteenth century, the Grimm brothers made the folktale fashionable, and for the first time collections of tales from many countries became popular. Story collections by Andrew Lang, Joseph Jacobs, and Charles Perrault became the rage, with one important difference: these stories were written down to be read, not told aloud to be heard. As the nineteenth century gave way to the twentieth, there was a revival of interest in storytelling. Spearheaded by children's librarians and schoolteachers, a new kind of storytelling evolved— one that was aimed specifically at children and connected to literature and reading. The form of literature most chosen by these librarians and teachers was the traditional folktale.

By the middle of the twentieth century, storytelling was seen as a way of exposing children to literature that they would not discover by themselves and of making written language accessible to those who could not read it by themselves. Storytelling became a method of promoting an understanding of other cultures and a means of strengthening the cultural awareness of the listening group. Current research confirms what librarians and teachers have known all along — that storytelling provides a practical, effective, and enjoyable way to introduce children to literature while fostering a love of reading.

Some of the most common themes appearing in folktales around the world deal with good overcoming evil; the clever outwitting the strong; and happiness being the reward for kindness to strangers, the elderly, and the less fortunate. We hear these themes repeated in stories from quaint Irish villages along the Atlantic coast to tiny communities spread throughout the African veldt and from cities and towns of the industrialized Americas to the magnificent palaces of the emperors of China and Japan. It is these similarities that are fascinating; that help us transcend the barriers of language, politics, custom, and religion; and that bind us together as "the folk" in folktales.

About the Story

Kao and the Golden Fish is a very popular story among Thai children. It is a tale of a mother's unending love. Although the story is set in the lush, tropical country of Thailand in Southeast Asia, in many ways it resembles the classic "Cinderella" story in western literature. A mother dies, the father remarries, and an unfriendly stepmother and her child are jealous of the beautiful daughter who eventually marries the prince of the land.

In the Thai version, however, there are important differences, which are based on a belief in reincarnation. Instead of a fairy godmother, Kao's benefactor is her deceased mother who returns to be with her first as a golden fish, then as an eggplant, and finally as two beautiful, towering trees. As a tribute to a mother's enduring love and a child's efforts to protect it, this story compels the child in each of us to believe in the eternal presence of love even when it appears most absent.

Because goldfish have been around for centuries, the presence of a goldfish as a central character in this folktale is significant. Ancient Japanese and Chinese artwork show that goldfish were kept in ponds and as household pets about 1,000 years ago and probably were exported extensively throughout Asia and Europe.

How to use this folktale book and audiocassette

The two components of the Adventures in Storytelling series — a wordless book and an audiocassette — have been carefully designed to promote the art of storytelling and should be used together. Because many folktales are not commonly known, we suggest that those who are learning or retelling the story for the first time listen to the story on tape while also following the illustrations in the book. After learning the story, tellers can use the pictures in the book to guide them in retelling the story from their own rich, ethnic perspective. For additional reference, the complete story text is printed in the back of the book. By using this wordless folktale book and the audiocassette, each listener will have an opportunity to enjoy literature, learn about other cultures, and develop oral language and prereading skills.

Long ago, a beautiful girl named Kao lived with her parents in a little village in Thailand. Although the family worked very hard, they were happy — until the day Kao's mother died.

Not long after her mother's death, Kao's father married again. The woman's name was Sang and her daughter's name was Sri. Sri was not as pretty as Kao, and she was lazy. Although Kao tried to get along with her stepmother and stepsister, it was not easy. They forced her to do all the work while they did nothing but find fault with her.

As the years passed, Kao's father became very old and sickly. Within a short time, he too died, leaving Kao feeling very sad and alone.

One day, when Kao went down to the lake in back of her house to bathe, a magical thing happened. While she was sitting at the edge of the lake, thinking about her mother and father, a beautiful golden fish swam to her. She tried to make the fish go away so it wouldn't get hurt while she was bathing, but it kept swimming close to her.

Kao bent down and was just about to touch the fish when she heard it say, "Kao, my lovely daughter, it is I, your mother. I know that you are unhappy and lonely so I have come back to visit with you."

Kao could not believe what she had heard. She moved closer to the fish and looked right into its eyes. "Mother," she said, "Could it be you?"

Just then, the fish began to swim away. As it left, it said, " I will wait for you here every morning, my darling daughter. Return to this spot and look for me."

So every morning of the following week, Kao went down to the lake to bathe. And every morning the golden fish was waiting for her. For hours they enjoyed each other's company.

But when Kao began staying at the lake longer every day, Sang became suspicious. She wondered why it was taking Kao so long to bathe and why she was so happy when she returned.

One morning, as Kao took her usual walk to the lake, Sang told Sri to follow her. Sri obeyed her mother and hid behind some bushes by the lake. When Sri saw and heard Kao talking to the golden fish, she ran home to tell Sang.

The next morning, at Sang's request, Sri dressed in Kao's clothing and went down to the lake before Kao arrived. She pretended to be Kao as she bent over the golden fish. Just as the fish was about to speak, Sri snatched it and ran quickly home.

When Kao arrived at the lake, the golden fish was nowhere to be seen. Even when she called to the fish, it did not appear. Saddened by her disappearance, Kao walked home. There, upon entering the house, Kao found Sang frying a golden fish. She was horrified by what she saw and ran from the house crying.

Kao waited for Sang and Sri to leave the house; then she returned. Carefully, she gathered the delicate fish bones and took them outside. As she buried them behind the house, she prayed that her mother would come back to her. Every day she watered the place where she had buried the bones. After several weeks, an eggplant began to grow there. Kao believed that this was the answer to her prayers: her mother had returned!

Every morning on the way back from the lake where she bathed, Kao would stop by the eggplant and talk to it. She was very happy again. But once again Sang had been watching Kao carefully. She was jealous of Kao's happiness. She did not want her to have more than Sri had. So, one morning, when Kao was down by the lake, Sang told Sri to pull out the eggplant that Kao had been caring for and bring it back to the house. Sri obeyed her mother.

When Kao returned, she was shocked to find that the eggplant had been uprooted. Immediately, she ran to the house. There, through the window, she saw Sang cooking an eggplant. Kao fell to her knees and began to cry. But as she sat beneath the window crying, she noticed that several seeds had fallen from the eggplant as it was being carried into the house.

Kao picked up the seeds and walked far away from the house. There, alongside the road, she planted them and prayed that her mother would come back to her. As often as she could, she returned to the place where she had buried the seeds. Eventually, two trees began to grow there.

For the next several months, Kao talked to the trees and watered them. As the years passed, travelers along the road sought comfort in the shade of the trees. They talked about the beautiful music they heard when the wind blew through the branches. When Kao sat beneath the trees, she could hear her mother's voice in the sweet music of the wind. She was comforted by the protection of the trees and the sound of her mother's voice.

One very hot day, a prince came by and stopped to rest in the shade of the two trees. He was very tired, and the music made by the wind in the trees made him fall asleep. When he awoke, he felt more happy and rested than he had ever felt before. He decided that he would have the trees brought to his palace grounds.

Upon returning to the palace, the prince ordered his soldiers to dig up the trees and bring them to him immediately. But when the soldiers tried to uproot the trees, they would not budge. So the next day, the soldiers returned with an elephant. But even the elephant could not move the trees. When the prince learned of this, he asked his soldiers to put up notices among the villagers, asking the owner

of the trees to come forward. After reading one of the notices, Kao set out for the palace.

When she arrived at the palace, Kao was immediatly brought to the prince. He asked her if she would allow him to plant the trees in the palace grounds. Kao wanted to help the prince and told him that she would be back the next day with an answer for him.

After leaving the palace, Kao went to visit her trees. Beneath their shade and the comfort of their music, Kao talked about the prince and his request. "It would make me happy to make the prince happy," she said. "Mother, will you let me take you to the palace? You will make both of us happy, and you will be safe."

As the wind gently rustled the leaves of the trees, Kao heard her mother's voice. "Yes, lovely Kao. I want you and the prince to be happy. Return here tomorrow with him and we will all go back to the palace together."

The next day, Kao returned with the prince. They placed their hands on the trees. Immediately, the trees began to move; then they fell. That same day the trees were planted on the palace grounds. There, under the comforting shade of the tall, green trees, the prince asked Kao to marry him. She said "yes" and never returned to Sang and Sri's home again. In time, Kao's stepmother and stepsister learned from the villagers how happy Kao was, living in the palace with the prince and comforted by the voice of her mother in the singing trees.

Acknowledgments
Project Editor: Alice Flanagan
Design and Electronic Page Composition: Biner Design
Engraver: Liberty Photoengravers
Printer: Lake Book Manufacturing, Inc.

About the Storytellers ——— About the Illustrator

My name is Wilai Punpattanakul-Crouch. I was born in the northern part of Thailand, in the little village of Kwuan Phayao, many years ago. My family loved to listen to the wonderful stories my grandfather told. The story of the golden fish, one of the many tales he liked to tell, is a favorite of mine. In Thailand it continues to be one of the most popular children's stories.

In 1975, I came to the United States to study education. After returning to Thailand, I taught English and mathematics in high school. I now live with my husband in Wagoner, Oklahoma.

Wilai Punpattanakul Crouch

My name is Cheryl Hamada. I am a *sansei* (a third generation Japanese American) and the storyteller you hear on the tape recording of *Kao and the Golden Fish.*

I live in Chicago, Illinois, where I am an actress and speech therapist. When I was a little girl, my brothers and sisters and I filled our play-time with make-believe. Instead of surrounding ourselves with toys, we pretended to be all the characters we imagined in our fantasies. After I learned to read, I read constantly. I don't think there was a fairytale or a folktale book in the library that I had not read several times. Now these happy childhood memories and imaginative moments continue to influence me as an adult.

I hope, as you listen to and retell the story of *Kao and the Golden Fish,* you will understand the timelessness of love. May all your childhood memories be happy ones.

Cheryl Hamada

I was only six years old in China when my father brought home a sketch book and gave it to me. It was then I knew I wanted to paint. At the age of twelve, I began studying art under special tutorship at home. Nine years later, I became an apprentice to Pu-Juh, one of the great modern masters of Chinese brush painting. Later, I continued my studies in Rome, Italy, and Brussels, Belgium.

Today, as a freelance artist and teacher, I frequently instruct students in Chinese brush painting in mainland China, Taiwan, Belgium, and at the Field Museum and Art Institute of Chicago, Illinois. Although my paintings have been exhibited and sold worldwide, making my paintings accessible to children is also very important to me. Illustrating the folktale *Kao and the Golden Fish* has allowed me to do this. I hope it will encourage children who are interested in art and storytelling to pursue their dreams.

Monica Liu

Library of Congress Cataloging-in-Publication Data
Wilai Punpattanakul-Crouch
    Kao and the golden fish : a folktale from Thailand / retold by Cheryl Hamada as remembered by Wilai Punpattanakul-Crouch; illustrated by Monica Liu.
        p.   cm. — (Adventures in storytelling)
        Summary: Pictures tell the story of a beautiful young girl who suffers at the hands of her jealous stepmother and stepsister. Text appears in the back of the book.
        ISBN 0-516-05145-8
    [1. Folklore — Thailand.] I. Punpattanakul-Crouch, Wilai. II. Liu, Monica, ill. III. Title. IV. Series.
PZ8.1.H1485Kao 1993   93-298
398.21—dc20   CIP
[E]   AC